The POKY LITTLE PUPPY
and the
PUMPKIN PATCH

By Diane Muldrow, after Janette Sebring Lowrey,
author of *The Poky Little Puppy*

Illustrated by Sue DiCicco

A GOLDEN BOOK • NEW YORK

One crisp fall morning, five little puppies
went for a walk.

Through the meadow they went, over the
bridge and across the green grass, one right
after the other. Along the way, they saw trees
full of red, orange, and yellow autumn leaves.

But when they got to the top of the hill, they counted themselves: *one, two, three, four.* One little puppy wasn't there.

"Where in the world is that poky little puppy?" they wondered.

When they looked down at the bottom of
the hill, there he was, looking at something
over on the next hill.

"I see something!" he called. "A bright red
tractor pulling a wagon!"

The other puppies saw it, too.

Over the hills they ran, as fast as they
could go.

"It's a hayride!" cried the puppies.
"Hop aboard," said the farmer. "I'm going
to visit the pumpkin patch!"

So the five little puppies jumped onto the
wagon and went for a ride. What fun! The air
was cool, and the sun was warm. They bumped
along past a cornfield and an apple orchard.

They stopped at a field with lots and lots of . . .

PUMPKINS!

"You may each choose a pumpkin to take home," said the farmer.

But which pumpkin? the puppies wondered. There were so many!

Suddenly, one of the puppies cried, "Let's roll in the hay!"

So the puppies jumped—roly poly, pell mell—into soft piles of hay.

Soon they were playing hide-and-seek.

Then they counted themselves: *one, two, three, four.*

Where in the world was the poky little puppy?

He had found a corn maze!

So the puppies trotted through the
maze as fast as they could go, heading
this way and that way . . .

until they made it out the other side: *one, two, three, four.*

Where was that poky little puppy *now*?

There he was, sniffing the air.
"I smell something!" said Poky.
The four little puppies began to sniff,
and they smelled it, too.
"Apple cider!" they cried.

The puppies soon found apple cider doughnuts to eat, and warm apple cider to drink!

They ate as much as they could, and then ran back to the pumpkin patch, one right after the other.

The puppies picked *one, two, three, four, five* pumpkins—all by themselves!

And home they went as fast as they could go, to carve their pumpkins.

After dinner, when the sun went down,
the puppies enjoyed their glowing jack-o'-lanterns
while they ate pumpkin pie for dessert.

The puppies were so tired!

But the poky little puppy was the last to fall asleep, because he couldn't stop thinking about the fun he'd had on their wonderful, pumpkin-picking autumn day.